谨以此书献给清华百年

本书出版得到清华大学亚洲研究中心（ARC）资助

中国西南
濒危文字图录

——清华百年西南濒危文字展选

Catalog of the Endangered Scripts in Southwest China

赵丽明　宋兆麟　编

Editor　Zhao Liming　Song Zhaolin

学苑出版社
Academy Press

图书在版编目（CIP）数据

中国西南濒危文字图录：清华百年西南濒危文字展选：汉英对照／赵丽明，宋兆麟编．－北京：学苑出版社，2011.4
ISBN 978-7-5077-3773-8

Ⅰ．①中… Ⅱ．①赵… ②宋… Ⅲ．①古文字－西南地区－图录 Ⅳ．① K877.92

中国版本图书馆 CIP 数据核字（2011）第 058288 号

出 版 人：孟　白
策　　划：刘　涟
责任编辑：洪文雄　　杨　雷
装帧设计：徐道会
出版发行：学苑出版社
社　　址：北京市丰台区南方庄 2 号院 1 号楼
邮政编码：100079
网　　址：www.book001.com
电子信箱：xueyuan@public.bta.net.cn
销售电话：010-67675512　67678944　67601101（邮购）
经　　销：新华书店
印 刷 厂：北京信彩瑞禾印刷厂
开本尺寸：787×1092　　1/16
印　　张：8
版　　次：2011 年 4 月第 1 版
印　　次：2011 年 4 月第 1 次印刷
定　　价：150.00 元

前　言

赵丽明

　　中国西南地区，包括川滇黔桂等地区。这里有著名的三江并流、茶马古道、藏彝走廊、南北丝绸之路，是各种文化交汇、传承多元文明的沃土。这里蕴藏了汉藏语乃至南亚语的宝贵资源，更是各种原始象形文字的富矿。

　　除东巴文外，这里曾活跃着汝卡、摩梭、普米、纳木依、耳苏、木雅、他留，以及坡芽歌书、水书、女书等诸多不同形态的文字。但随着岁月的流失、社会的发展，这些曾与当地人民群众生产生活息息相关的古老文字，目前仅依附在少数传承人身上，大多已处于濒危状态，且能全部识读、解读的人已寥寥无几。尽管如此，在西南的大山和老林里，这些文字还在顽强生存着。

　　中国有悠久的历史和文化，其中汉字从哪里来，是大家关心的问题之一。西南民族地区保留有各种活态的原始文字的命题，前人做了大量的工作，在此基础上，我们又多次赴川滇地区，侧重考察中国文字的起源。结果发现，当地还有不少的祭司还在使用图画和象形文字书写的经书，有的也普及到一般民众。这些图画和象形文字，是在原始的刻划和绘画基础上衍生、发展的。因此，这些文献及其文字为我们展示了文字是如何从图画到文字的发生学过程。

如同西亚的两河流域、北非的尼罗河流域、中国的黄河流域和长江流域乃至淮河流域，也是古文明的发祥地。自甲骨文发现以来，各地陆续出土数十种史前文字符号。它们和汉字有什么关系？能否为汉字的起源提供可靠、有序的发生学链条？即汉字是怎样产生的？如何起源的？这些问题，是人们，特别是学术界所关心的难题。

也许，本书中所汇集资料，会给我们一个启示，一条探索的途径，一个较为清晰的答案。

本书中所归集的濒危文字的共同点是：他们都是土生土长的、都是为了记录使用者的认知、行为、情感而产生的。其特点主要有：

1、多为原始阶段的图符文字、象形文字，不能完整记录语言。

2、多与图画、图符混合使用，字与画的界限尚处模糊、过渡阶段。

3、传承处于断裂状态，大多仅存极少数人（多为祭司）能识读、释读，有的几乎无人能全面解读。

4、大多仍被祭司在当地群众的日常生活中使用，与生产生活密切相关，坚强地残存于民间。

5、表现形态多元化：史前文字符号、文字画；原始图画文字、图符文字、象形文字，语段文字、音节文字、音素文字；自源的、借源的。

这些文字，它们尽管濒危，但还活着；这些传承人，他们贫困着，但守望着、执着着、热衷着、传承着；他们在那绵延不断的青藏高原、云贵高原交界处的横断山脉，在那湍急澎湃、奔腾不息的金沙江、澜沧江、怒江、雅砻江、大渡河的峡谷，在那悠然的白云、高高的蓝天、远远的雪山下，伴随着茶马古道的轻扬铃声，在汉文化、藏文化、氐羌文化、越文化的古今交汇带上，固守那份虔诚、那份纯净、那份安宁。这里保护了华夏生命之水，也保存了文明之源、人类的孩提时代。

庆幸的是，我们找到了一个宝库，她是人类文明母体活样板，是目前全人类独有的文字产生的活态博物馆。在现代文明的冲击下，她很弱势，需要我们关心她、呵护她；她也要生存、也要发展。如何挖掘、整理、抢救、解读、保护、传承、开发，这对非物质文化遗产保护提出了最迫切的课题。

清华大学有着辉煌的人文传统。不但传承文献、开创考古，而且走进田野。王国维、梁启超、赵元任、李方桂、李济、陈寅恪、朱自清、闻一多、刘盼遂、刘文典、吕叔湘、唐兰、王力、杨树达、高亨、季羡林、姜亮夫、徐中舒、许国璋、朱德熙、董同龢、张琨、朱芳圃、刘节、王还、戴家祥、张清常、马衡、王静如、马肇椿、陈乃雄、李学勤、黄昌宁、谢国桢、李赋宁等。这长长的名单，是清华百年人文脚印。

清华百年，人文日新。求实、求是、创新的人文传统，将王国维先生提出的传世文献、地下考古的"二重证据法"，加上地上民间考古，发展为"三重证据"。面对这个文字产生的活态博物馆，我们要抢在这些人类文明成果消失之前，走进去、挖出来，静下心，用科学方法记录、解读它。于是有了国家重大社科基础研究项目"中国西南地区濒危文字抢救、解读、整理与研究"。作为项目承担者的清华学子走进西南，关注、抢救、挖掘、收集濒危文字文献，并用所学知识，进行这些文字的整理、翻译、解读、数字化工作，如彝文、水书、女书等。

近些年我们发现了更多的仍生存于川滇藏偏僻山区的藏族、彝族、蒙古族、纳西族、普米族、傈僳族以及各民族支系摩梭、汝卡、尔苏、木雅、纳木依、他留等族群使用的民间文献，并走访了其传承人，有了初步研究成果，其中多项目多次获国家部委奖项（彝族古文献、女书等）、清华大学科研挑战杯特等奖（水书、版纳文身项目等）。

恰逢清华百年校庆，我们举办了"清华百年西南濒危文字展"，我们特选择中国西南各民族或民族支系部分代表性的文献材料编成此图录，力求勾勒出这些濒危文字的分布和基本概况，让社会各界来关注这些濒危的中华文化遗产。这也是清华学子辛苦汗水的结晶，是我们迈出的第一步。任重道远，我们会更加努力！

2011 年 3 月 22 日晨于清华园蓝旗营

Preface

Zhao Liming

China has a long-standing history with rich cultures. One of the most engaging topics is the origin of the Chinese characters. Southwest China roughly consists of Sichuan, Yunnan, Guizhou Provinces and Guangxi Zhuang Autonomous Region. Intertwined with the Three Parallel Rivers, the Ancient Tea Route, Tibetan-Yi Corridor, southern and northern Silk Road, the region embodies the hubs of multiform cultures and diverse civilizations that have been inherited and passed on from generation to generation. It also serves as a bonanza of Sino-Tibetan and South Asian language families, including proto-pictographs.

Besides Dongba scripts, there are many more types of scripts in this region, including the scripts of the ethnic minority groups and their branches such as Ruka, Mosuo, Pumi, Namuzi, Ersu, Muya, Taliu, and Poya Geshu (Poya Folk script), Shuishu (script of Shui people), Nüshu(script of Jiangyong women), and so on. However, as time went by and the society kept on developing, these ancient scripts, once closely related to the native people, become scarcely used by the following generations. Most of the scripts are on the verge of extinction, and only few people can read, explain and interpret them. Fortunately, things are not necessarily hopeless. These scripts continue to exist in the high mountains and old forests of Southwest China. For us, it is an urgent task to explore, collate, salvage, interpret, protect, pass on and develop these intangible cultural heritages, namely these endangered writing systems.

Tsinghua University has a magnificent academic tradition of the humanities, in which the scholars have gathered and preserved valuable manuscripts and archives, established the discipline of Chinese archeology, did important field work and are currently leading information processing in the modern era: Wang Guowei, Liang Qichao, Chao Yuen Ren, Li Fang-Kuei, Li Ji, Chen Yinke, Zhu Ziqing, Wen Yiduo,

Liu Pansui, Liu Wendian, Lu Shuxiang, Tang Lan, Wang Li, Yang Shuda, Gao Heng, Ji Xianlin, Jiang Liangfu, Xu Zhongshu, Xu Guozhang, Zhu Dexi, Dong Tonghe, Zhang Kun, Zhu Fangpu, Liu Jie, Wang Huan, Dai Jiaxiang, Zhang Qingchang, Ma Heng, Wang Jingru, Ma Zhaochun, Chen Naixiong, Li Xueqin, Huang Changning, Xie Guozhen, Li Funing. This long list functions as an impressive footprint of Tsinghua's achievements of the humanities in the past hundred years.

The past century has witnessed daily renewal of success in Tsinghua University, In the process of seeking reality, truth and creation in the humanities. The Double Evidence Approach put forward by Mr. Wang Guowei has been advanced to the Triple Evidence Approach to the combination of the classical documents and the archaeological studies with folk discovery. Inspired by the ecological musiems where the pictographic writings were produced, the students from Tsinghua University visited the southwest part of China. Hence the significant project of national social sciences is listed under the title of *the Endangered Scripts in Southwest China: Saving, Interpreting, Collating and Researching*.

Aimed at the origin of the Chinese writing systems, our team has done extensive fieldwork research in the area of Sichuan, Yunnan and Tibet. In our research, we found that some endangered scripts are still alive within ethnic groups of the Tibetans, the Yis, the Mongolians, the Naxis, the Pumis, the Lisus and some of their branches including the Mosuo people, the Ruka people, the Ersu people, the Muya people, the Namuzi people and the Taliu people inhabited in the remote mountainous areas. Written with pictographs and hieroglyphs, scriptures were substantial among local priests, some of which were also in populace use. These symbolic writings and scripts were derived from Primitive carvings and paintings, thus offering us major examples of phylogeny and revealing how the written forms evolved from pictographs.

The native endangered scripts have been used to record people's thoughts, behavior and emotions. They have the following features:

1. Most of them are icons or hieroglyphs at the Primitive stage, that cannot be used to completely record the speeches it belongs to;

2. They are mostly mixed with pictures and icons. The boundaries between the script and picture are vague;

3. Their inheritance is broken up, only a small number of the natives can read or decipher the remaining scripts but the rest are unintelligible;

4. The scripts are mostly used by the priests for the local people and daily life, thus remaining useful in the local community;

5. Diversity: the scripts consisted of drawings, grapheme (glyphs referring to a paragraph of sentences), primitive pictographic writing, pictographic writing, hieroglyph, phrase writing, syllabic writing, phonemic language, self-derivation writing and loan writing.

In order to collect and save the endangered scripts, we visited the native users. Progress has been made in the their arrangement, translation, deciphering and digitalizing. Some sub-projects have more than once won awards from national ministries (Yi ancient literatures, Nüshu, etc.), or the Grand Prize in Challenge Cup of Tsinghua University (Shuishu, Traditional tattoos in Xishuangbanna Prefecture, etc.). The Catalog demonstrates the distribution and the current situation of the endangered scripts after years of hard work. It is merely our first step, and we still have a rather long way to go.

Lanqiying, Tsinghua University, Beijing

March 22, 2011, a.m.

目 录

前 言 /1

一、纳西族 /1

俄亚东巴文 /2
俄亚东巴画 /3
俄亚占卜经 /8
汝卡东巴文 /14
白地汝卡《祈福经》/15
油米汝卡《祭祖经》/18
汝卡印棒 /22
哥巴文 /24
《色可多撒》经 /25
宝山东巴文 /26
东巴文《会议记录》/27
东巴文《土地买卖契约》/28
摩梭达巴文 /30
摩梭历书《哥里木》/31
达巴文《格木经》抄本 /32
达巴文《格木经》彩绘本 /33
达巴印棒 /35

二、普米族 /36

汉规历书《夏多吉吉》/37
普米印棒 /41

三、藏　族 /42

耳苏沙巴文 /43
沙巴文《母虎历书》/43
沙巴经书 /46

纳木依帕孜经书 /50

帕孜《送魂经》/51

纳木依历书 /56

纳木依印棒 /61

木雅经书 /62

木雅历书 /63

打卦图 /66

四、彝　族 /70　　**毕摩文献** /70

修复后的毕摩文献 /70

未修复的毕摩文献 /71

他留铎系文 /73

灵牌上的铎系文 /73

五、壮　族 /74　　坡芽歌书 /75

六、傈僳族 /76　　**汪忍波音节文字** /77

汪忍波音节文字抄本 /77

七、水　族 /80　　**水书** /81

水书抄本 /81

八、附　录 /85　　**女书** /85

婚嫁时的礼物三朝书 /86

太平天国女书铜币 /87

女书作品（一）/88

女书作品（二）/88

鸣　谢 /89

Contents

I. The Naxis / 1

The Eya Dongba Scripts / 2
Paintings of the Eya Dongba / 3
The Eya Sacred Books / 8
The Ruka Dongba Scripts / 14
The Ruka *Blessing Scripture* in Baidi / 15
The Ruka *Ancestors Worshipping Scriptures* in Youmi / 18
The Rukas' Yin Bang / 22
The Geba Scripts / 24
Scripture: *Se Ke Do Sa* / 25
The Baoshan Dongba Scripts / 26
Meeting Record in the Dongba Scripts / 27
Legal Documents of Land Dealings in the Dongba Scripts / 28
The Daba Scripts of the Mosuo People / 30
Gelimu :the Almanac of the Mosuo People / 31
The Hand-copied Dabas' *Gemu Classics* / 32
The Colored Dabas' *Gemu Classics* / 33
The Dabas' Yin Bang / 35

II. The Pumis / 36

The Pumi Almanac *Shia Do Ji Ji* / 37
The Pumi Yin Bang / 41

III. The Tibetans / 42

The Shaba Scripts of the Ersu People / 43
The Almanac of Tigress / 43
Scripture of Ersu Shaba / 46

The Pazi Pictographs of the Namuzi People / 50

The Pazis' *Itinerary Map* / 51

The Almanac of the Namuzi People / 58

The Namuzis' Yin Bang / 61

The Muyas' Scriptures / 62

The Almanac of the Muya People / 63

The Divination Painting / 66

IV. The Yis / 70

Bimo Documents / 70

Restored Bimo Documents / 70

Original Bimo Documents / 71

The Duoxi Scripts of the Taliu People / 73

The Duoxi Scripts on Spirit Tablets / 73

V. The Zhuangs / 74

The Poya Geshu / 75

VI. The Lisus / 76

Wang Renbo Syllabic Characters / 77

The Hand-copied Wang Renbo Syllabic Characters / 77

VII. The Shuis / 80

Shuishu / 81

The Hand-copied Version of Shuishu /81

VIII. Appendix / 85

Nüshu / 85

Sanzhao Shu, the Gift for Marriage / 86

The Nüshu Copper Coin of Taiping Heavenly Kingdom / 87

Nüshu Script I / 88

Nüshu Script II / 88

Acknowledgements / 89

一、纳西族

纳西族东巴文知名度较高，但纳西族众多支系所衍生出的东巴文姊妹文种却鲜为人知。除云南丽江之外，纳西族还生活在三江并流的高山峡谷之中，跨滇川藏区。这一带在历史上是藏文化、原始文化、汉文化交汇之地，是茶马古驿道由滇进藏的咽喉，中国明代地理学家徐霞客游历的终点也是这里。或许正是由于徐霞客在此的戛然而止，冥冥之中才引来了洛克等外国人的目光。

纳西族各支系所处地理偏僻、交通不便，至今比较完好地保存了多彩多姿的原生态文化，其中就有由众多的东巴文姊妹文种形成的东巴文体系。

I. The Naxis

The script of the Naxi Dongba is a famous one, but the numerous branches are barely known. Due to the isolation of the geographic environment and inconvenience of transportation, the Naxi's colorful original cultures are well preserved. This includes the script system which is comprised of many of the relevant scripts.

俄亚东巴文

　　俄亚，位于川西南尽头，今属四川省木里县，这里有著名的纳西"俄亚大村"。去俄亚，尚不能按常规进川走木里县城，而要从云南香格里拉进入，尽可能地驱车到海拔近4000米的大山脚下，然后还要在山路上艰难跋涉两天。

　　俄亚纳西族信仰原始宗教，每逢节日、婚丧嫁娶、求雨等重要活动，东巴都要进行诵经、占卜、跳神等宗教仪式。东巴使用一种象形文字记载经书事项，故称之为东巴文。在俄亚用东巴文写的东巴文献种类很多，主要有龙王经、祭风经、超度经、退口舌是非经、占卜经、除秽经、丧葬经等。

The Eya Dongba scripts

Eya is situated in the remote corner of the southwest of Sichuan Province, which belongs to Muli Tibetan Autonomous County where the famous "Grand Village of Eya" of the Naxi is located. The villagers are believers of a primitive religion, the scriptures of which are written in the Dongba scripts by the priests so named. There are documents written in the Dongba script, such as the scriptures of Dragon King, Wind Sacrifice, Soul Releasing From the Suffering, Divination, Removing Dirty Sediments, and Funeral, etc.

俄亚东巴画

东巴在举行宗教活动时，经常使用一些小型彩绘绘画，主要内容有东巴神像、动物神和藏传佛教的神祇。一般保存不用，只在进行祭祀时取出来，事后再供奉。

Paintings of the Eya Dongba

During the religious activities, small colorful paintings are demonstrated with local idols, sacred animals, and Tibetan Buddhist gods.

俄亚占卜经

　　东巴有许多占卜方法，写成东巴经者也不少。其中有一种小方格东巴经，共22张，每张前边有一个神灵符号，其余为东巴文，它相当于一种挂签。在每张上方拴一根线，问卜者取一根线，然后东巴根据该线所系经页，进行解释。

The Eya Sacred Books

They are Dongba scriptures containing 22 sheets with small panes. A symbol of God is painted on the head of every sheet, and filled with the Dongba scripts. These sheets are regarded as fortune lots tied with a string for priests to draw on and interpret accordingly.

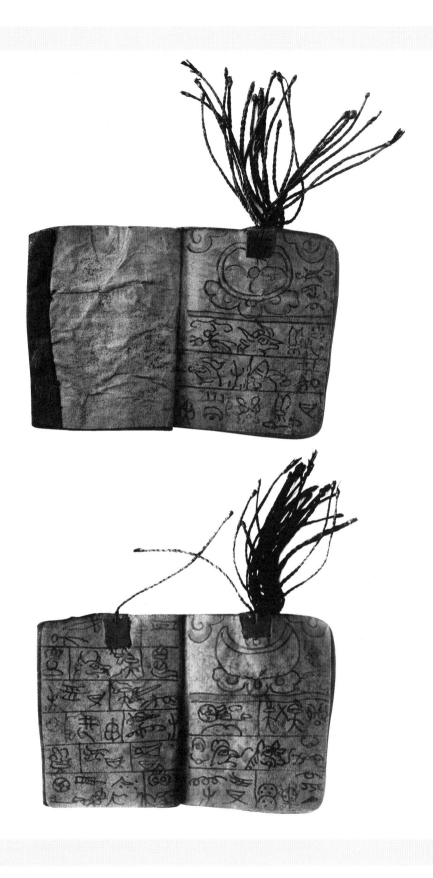

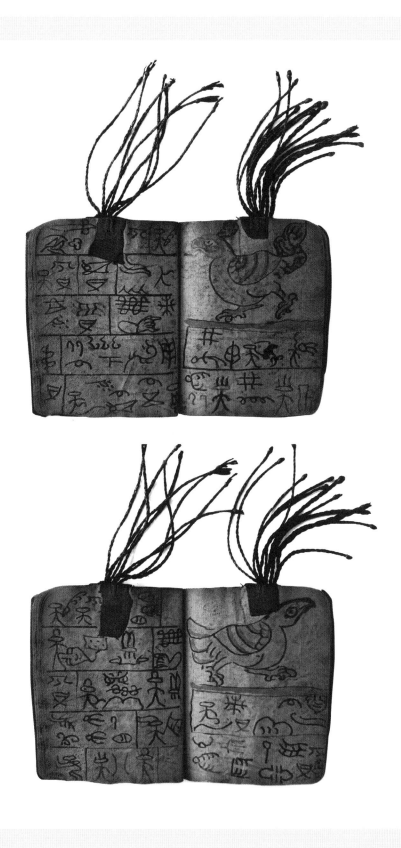

汝卡东巴文

　　汝卡，又称阮可。纳西汝卡人分布于川滇交界地区。汝卡人根据自己的方言，另造了一些字来记录本地一些语言的读音，因而产生了汝卡文。汝卡文是东巴文的变体，95% 以上的汝卡文与东巴文是一致的。汝卡文本身又因所处地域的不同，在字形上也有所不同。

The Ruka Dongba scripts

Ruka, also known as Ruanke, is distributed along the border of Sichuan and Yunnan provinces. According to the local dialects, the Ruka people use written forms to mark the pronunciation, hence the Ruka scripts came into being. They are variants of the Dongba scripts, with more than 95% being similar to the Dongba scripts. The formation of the scripts varies according to geographical conditions.

白地汝卡《祈福经》

  白地,是云南香格里拉县三坝乡的一个行政村。相传这里是东巴文化的发祥地,被称作"东巴圣地",民间有"不到白地不算是真正的东巴"的说法。这里至今保存有白水台和加威灵洞等纳西古迹。这里的纳西族自称"汝卡"。这部汝卡文《祈福经》讲的是为死者招魂祈福的仪式和追溯他们祖先的迁徙路线。

The Ruka *Blessing Scripture* in Baidi

Baidi is an administrative village in Sanba Township, Xianggelila County of Yunnan Province. The Naxi people here call themselves "the Rukas". Ruka's *Blessing Scripture* is used to summon the spirits of the dead and also trace the path that their ancestors followed.

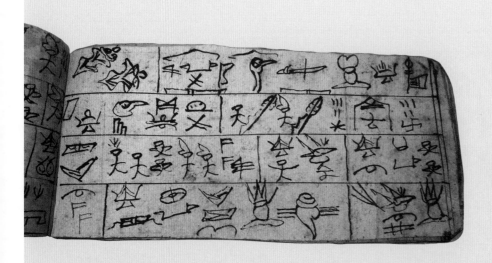

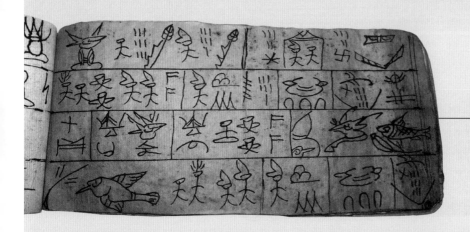

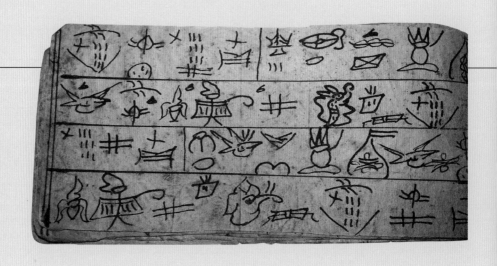

油米汝卡《祭祖经》

　　油米位于金沙江通天河段峡谷中的半山腰上。去油米，乘车只能到宁蒗县拉伯乡的加泽行政村，然后要翻越几座大山才能到达，山路上下坡度五六十度，人和马只能踩着石头缝隙前进。在这样的汝卡人山村里，完整地、全民性地保留着自己的文化。村里的男人个个认得东巴文，每到过年家家念诵《祭祖经》。

The Ruka *Ancestors Worshipping Scriptures* in Youmi

Youmi is in the Jinsha River Valley, the middle of the hillside of Tongtian . In Youmi, every man can read the *Ancestors Worshipping Scriptures*. During the New Year celebrations the prayer is performed as the sound conservation of their traditional culture.

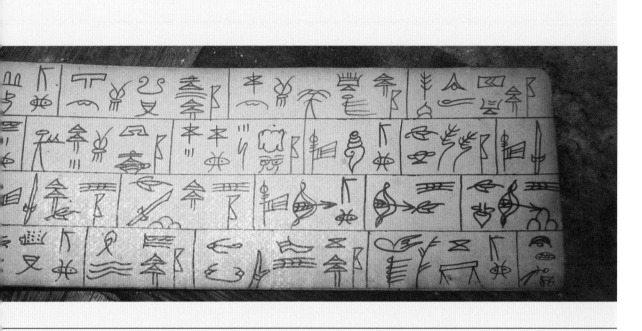

汝卡印棒

　　印棒，是做祭祀用面偶的模子。印棒上的各种符号，有汝卡人所崇拜的山神、水神等各种原始神明，也有各种人物、动物，还有各种邪恶魔鬼。这些符号代表着固定物体，有固定的读音，有的还与经书咒语相呼应、相配合。

The Rukas' Yin Bang

The wood molds known as *Yin Bangs* for making flour idols, are used for religious service. The icons on the Yin Bang depict ancient mountain gods and river gods that are being worshiped by the Ruka People. They also depict human beings, animals and devils symbolized with fixed objects in specific pronounciation, corresponding to the incantations used in the scriptures.

哥巴文

　　哥巴，是纳西语"弟子"的意思，哥巴文为东巴文的晚辈、后学。东巴文是原始文字向象形文字发展演变的动态过程，已经体现了六书规律；而哥巴文则是更加简化、抽象化，并沿着假借方向跨越进化。东巴文约有1500个字符，哥巴文只有约400个字符，大大减少了字符数量。哥巴文在文字发展史上，与东巴文一样具有重要的价值。纳西族经书在书写上，既有东巴文、哥巴文的混合经书，也有哥巴文专文经书。

The Geba scripts

Derived from the Dongba, the Geba script means the "disciple" in the Naxi. The entire script system, which is quite simple and abstract, has around 400 characters. In the history of its development, the Geba script is as valuable as Dongba script. It can be a mixed with the Dongba and Geba scripts, or specifically used in the sacred books.

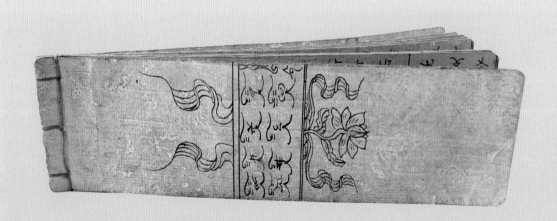

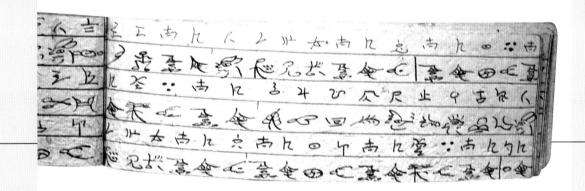

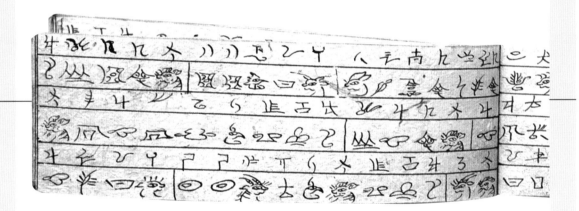

《色可多撒》经

　　《色可多撒》是哥巴文和东巴文对照书写的经书，是研究纳西象形文字发展演变不可多得的文献。

Scripture: *Se Ke Do Sa*

Se Ke Do Sa is a bilingual book of the Dongba and the Geba systems, a significant document in the research of the Naxi hieroglyphic development.

宝山东巴文

　　宝山是云南省丽江市玉龙县的一个乡。这里曾盛行东巴文化，至今仍保存大量用东巴文书写的文书。东巴文书的大量出现，说明东巴文已经突破宗教的功能，普及于民间百姓的日常生活，用于记录会议、土地交易等。但从 20 世纪后半叶开始，东巴文逐渐淡出该地历史舞台。

The Baoshan Dongba Scripts

Baoshan, a village in Yulong County of Lijiang, Yunnan Province, was dominated by Dongba culture. Therefore, many documents in Dongba scripts have been well preserved there. The Dongba script was prevalent among the local people, used to make meeting minutes and legal documents of land dealings. The Dongba script was in use before the late 20th century.

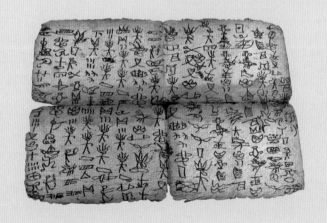

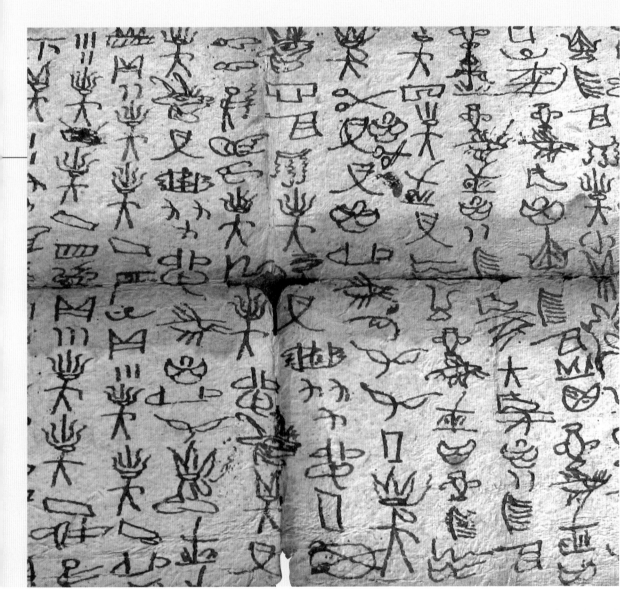

東巴文《土地買卖契约》
Legal Documents of Land Dealings in the Dongba scripts

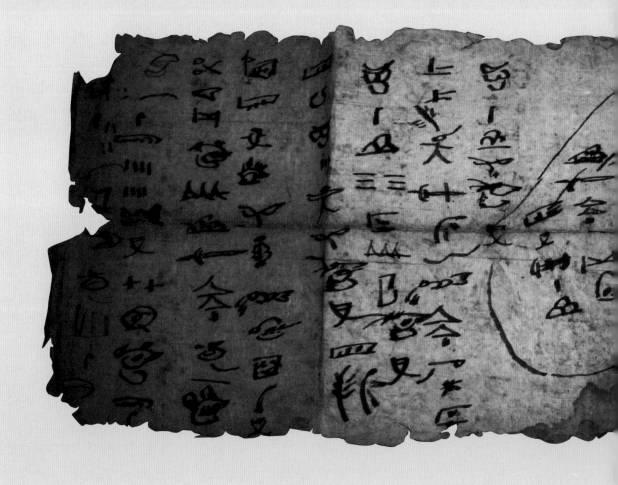

摩梭达巴文

　　摩梭人为纳西族的一支，主要分布在云南宁蒗永宁、四川盐源左所、四川木里屋脚等地。该族信仰达巴教。宗教祭司为达巴。达巴拥有丰富的口诵经文，并用一种象形文字记载经文。这种文字符号图案较之东巴文更加抽象、简化，有相对固定的含义、读音，并由摩梭达巴口耳相传，故被称作达巴文。

　　《格木经》是目前发现的摩梭祭司达巴最主要的书面经典，其功能大约同于汉族的历书，用于择日做事。《格木经》共 12 页，每页一个月，每月共 28 格或 30 格，每格一天，一年 336 天或 360 天。每格有两三个象形文字，表达该日的吉凶祸福。摩梭达巴的印棒也是各种各样，有两面、四面、六面、八面之别。

The Daba Scripts of the Mosuo people

The Mosuo people, as a branch of the Naxis, spreads mainly in Yongning Township of Ninglang County in Yunnan Province, Zuosuo Township of Yanyuan County and Wujiao Township of Muli County in Sichuan Province, etc. Mosuo people believe in Dabaism. The priests of Dabaism are called "Daba". They possess a great collection of the prayer books and pass them on orally from generation to generation.

Gemu Classics are the most important scriptures of the Daba that have been discovered so far. They are used for selecting lucky days for activities. The icons in Daba almanacs are more abstract and simpler compared with those in the Dongba scripts, and they have relatively fixed meanings and pronunciaitions. Each *Gemu Classic* consists of 12 pages. Each page stands for one month, and is divided into 28 or 30 small squares, each of which represents a day. The whole year has 336 or 360 days. Two or three hieroglyphic symbols written in one frame indicates what should or should not be done, or try to avoid that day. There are different types of Daba Yin Bangs (the wood molds for making flour idols). They can be of two, four, six or eight facets.

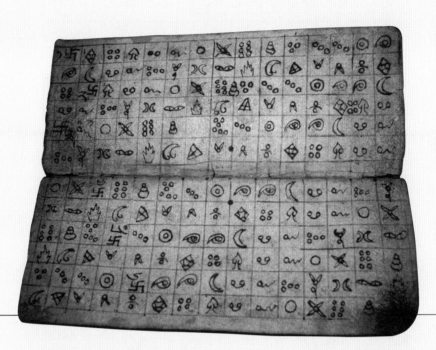

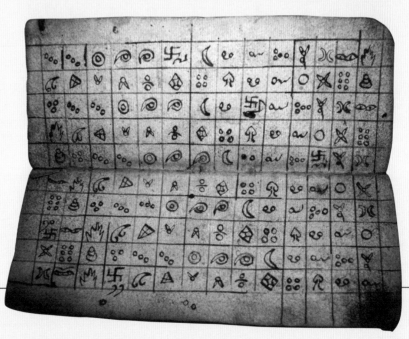

摩梭历书《哥里木》

Gelimu : **the Almanac of the Mosuo People**

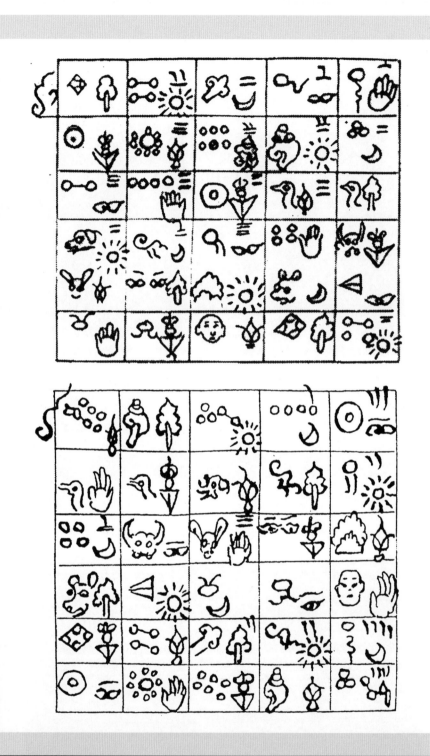

达巴文《格木经》抄本

The Hand-copied Dabas' *Gemu Classics*

达巴文《格木经》彩绘本

The Colored Version of the Dabas' *Gemu Classics*

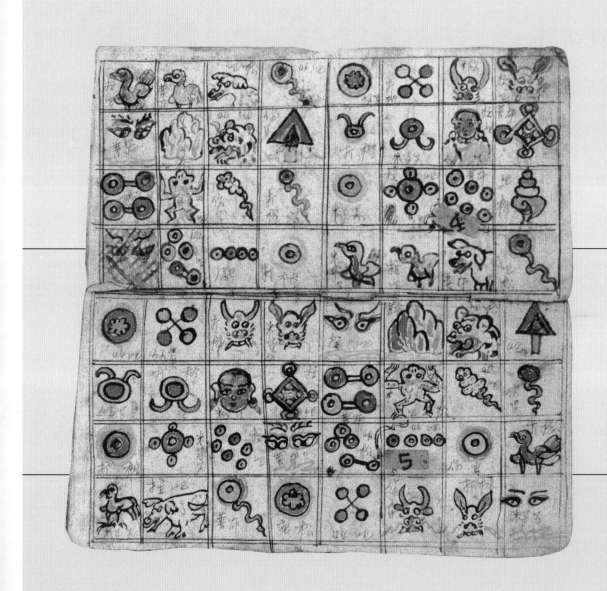

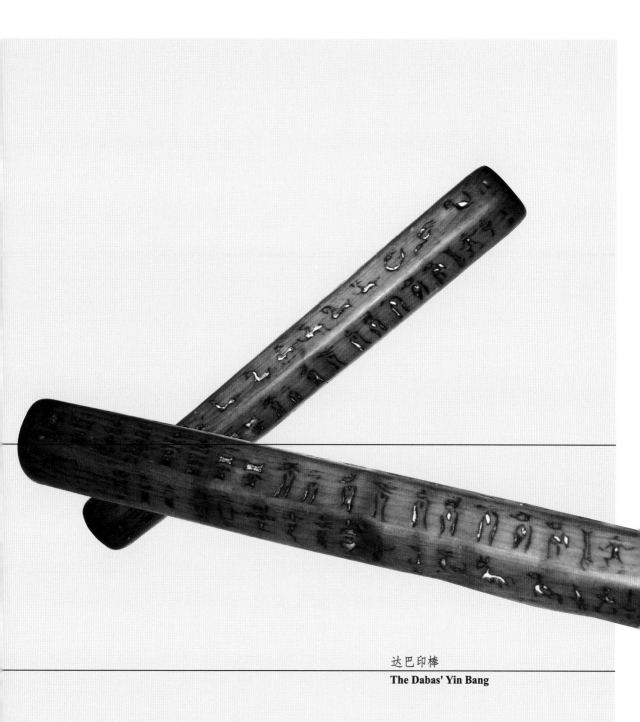

达巴印棒
The Dabas' Yin Bang

二、普米族

　　普米族主要散居在金沙江峡谷、横断山脉中，今云南兰坪、丽江、维西、永胜、宁蒗和四川木里、盐源等地，大约有两三万人。普米族的祭司称作汉规，他们使用一种图画文字记载宗教仪式等。汉规将祭祀的顺序和内容用图画或用藏文记载下来，并用以记载经文。在四川木里的依吉一带，完好地保存了100余种汉规经书文献。

II. The Pumis

The Pumis mainly inhabit in the Jinsha River Canyon and the Hengduan Mountains, in Lanping, Lijiang, Weixi, Yongsheng, Ninglang of Yunnan Province, and Muli and Yanyuan of Sichuan Province. The Population is about 20,000 to 30,000. The local priests are known as Hangui. In the area of Yiji, a township of Muli County in Sichuan Province, there are more than 100 well preserved Pumi scriptures.

汉规历书《夏多吉吉》
The Pumi almanac *Shia Do Ji Ji*

《夏多吉吉》是目前所见最丰富、最完善的汉规历书。每个月前面有小序，整部历书后面有注释说明。书中既有象形符号，又有藏文解释，恰好说明象形符号表情达意记录语言的不足，于是借用当地强势文化的藏文拼音字母来补充。

Shia Do Ji Ji is the richest and most comprehensive Pumi almanac discovered so far. The book has not only pictographic symbols, but also Tibetan explanations.

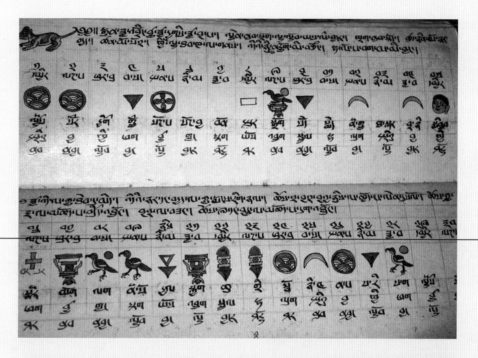

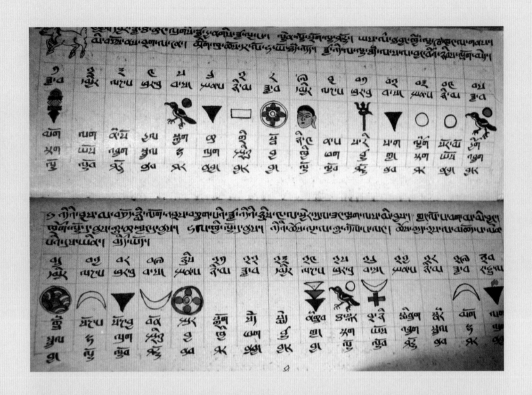

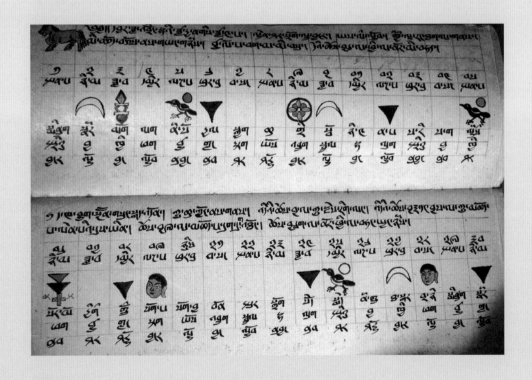

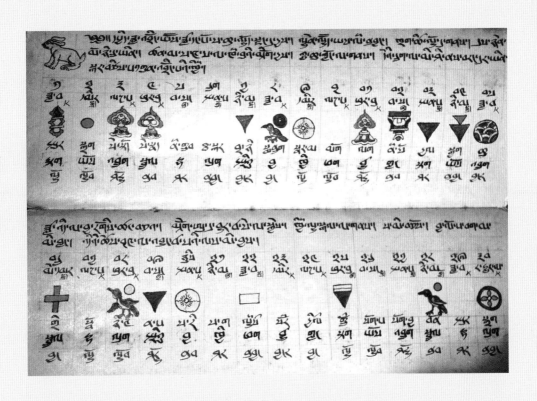

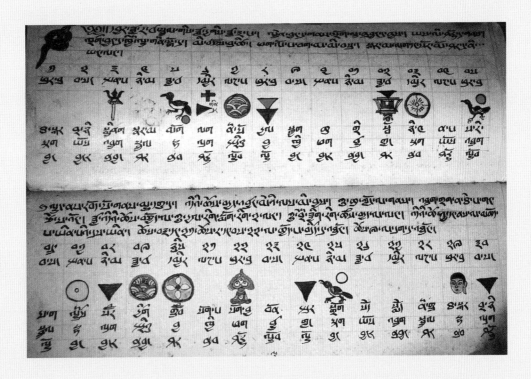

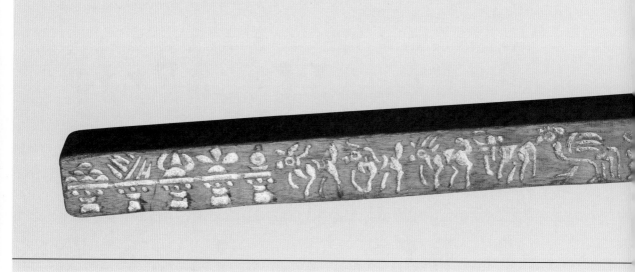

普米印棒
The Pumi Yin Bang

三、藏族

藏族是一个具有悠久历史和灿烂文化的民族。由于藏族居住地域辽阔，各地区藏族呈现出各具特色的地方方言和文化风俗，形成了若干个支系，除卫藏藏族、安多藏族、康巴藏族等传统藏族三大支系外，还有嘉绒藏族、白马藏族、纳木依藏族、尔苏藏族、木雅藏族等分支。

III. The Tibetans

The Tibetan people have a long history and a splendid culture. Due to their vast land the dialects and customs in each district are so specific and diversified that they have formed different ethnic sub-groups. Besides Central-Tibetan, Khampa, Amdo, there are Rgyal Rong, Bai Ma, Namuzi, Ersu, Muya (Min-Yag) and other sub-groups.

耳苏沙巴文

　　耳苏人为藏族支系之一，主要分布在川西南大渡河、安宁河、雅砻江流域的甘洛、越西、九龙、木里、冕宁、汉源、石棉一带。其语言属于汉藏语系藏缅语族羌语支，又分为三个方言区：东部方言耳苏、中部方言多续、西部方言里汝。沙巴文是继东巴文之后，在 20 世纪 80 年代被世人所知的一种文字。最早的报告者、研究者为刘尧汉、宋兆麟、严汝娴、孙宏开等先生。

The Shaba Scripts of the Ersu people

The Ersu people, as a sub-group of the Tibetans, live in the area of Dadu River and Anning River in southwestern Sichuan as well as Ganluo, Yuexi, Jiulong, Muli, Mianning, Hanyuan and Shimian in the Yalong River basin. The Shaba scripts was discovered in the 1980s following the discovery of the Dongba scripts.

沙巴文《母虎历书》

The Almanac of Tigress

　　耳苏人沙巴文经书曾很多，但目前已经处于极度濒危状态，民间自然传承凤毛麟角，能完全解读经书的祭司沙巴更是难以寻找。《母虎历书》又称《虐曼史达》，是耳苏沙巴择日的历书，以十二生肖纪月，虎月为首，因此得名。

Shaba, the priest of the Ersu people, selects auspicious days according to the *Almanac of Tigress*. Each month in the almanac is named after one animal of the Chinese zodiac, in which the tigress ranks first. That is how the almanac got its name.

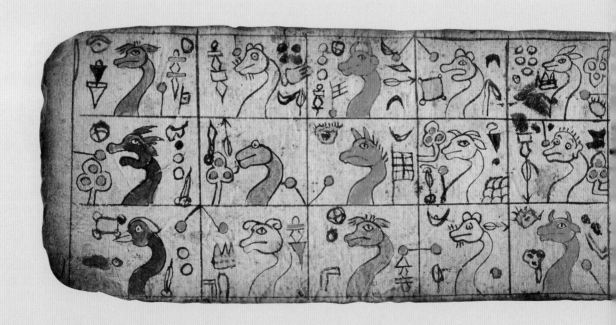

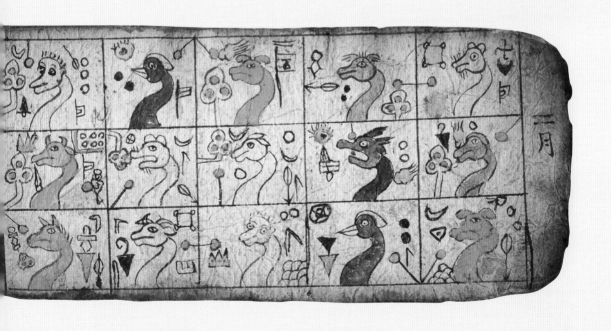

沙巴经书

Scripture of Ersu Shaba

2007 年搜集于四川省凉山州甘洛县沙岱乡日坡村。

Collected in Ripo Village in Shadai Township of
Ganluo County, Liangshan Yi Autonomous Prefecture,
Sichuan Province, in 2007.

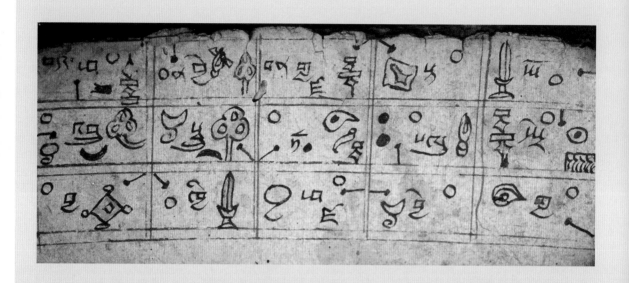

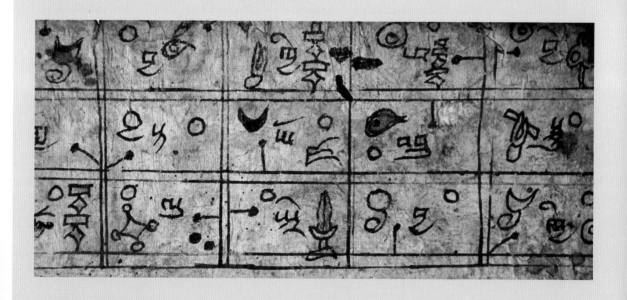

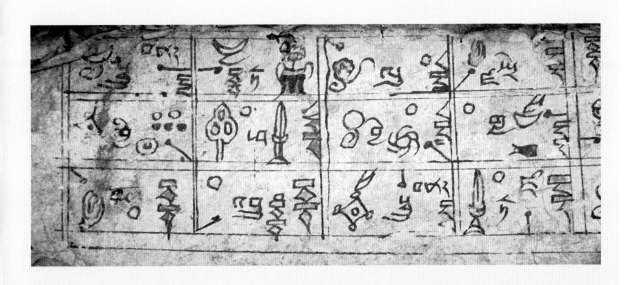

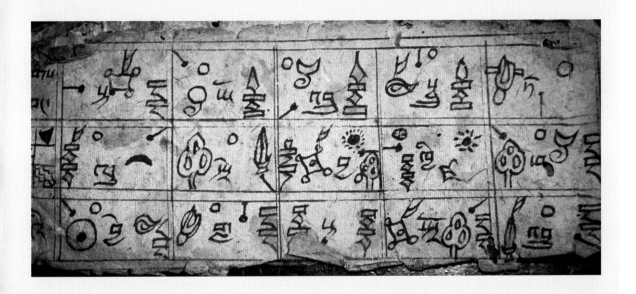

纳木依帕孜经书

纳木依（纳木兹）人，族群自称。纳，意为"黑"，木依（木兹），意为"人"，纳木依，意即黑人。纳木依人为藏族支系之一，主要分布于四川凉山州的冕宁、西昌、盐源、木里和甘孜州的九龙县，人口约 5000 人。学界一般认为纳木依语属于汉藏语系藏缅语族羌语支。

纳木依人信仰原始宗教，其祭司称帕孜（帕比）。纳木依人的宗教文化是由历书、经卷中的一幅幅五颜六色的图案记载下来的。这些图案由特定的图符组合而成，表达不同的含义，内容丰富多变。单独看图案，是不能理解其中要义的，要靠祭司帕孜解读。其传承靠师徒代代口传心授。帕孜经书中的图案为图画文字，有特定的发音、意义和用途，但与成熟的文字有很大的差别，可以看成人类文字的萌芽阶段。

The Pazi Pictographs of the Namuzi people

As one of the Tibetan ethnic sub-groups, the Namuzi people live in Mianning, Xichang, Yanyuan and Muli in Liangshan Yi Autonomous Prefecture as well as Jiulong County in Garze Tibetan Autonomous Prefecture, Sichuan Province. They are believers of a Primitive religion cared about by the priests known as "pazi" ("pabi"). The culture of the Namuzi people is recorded in a almanacs and sacred books with colourful paintings, only the pazi are qualified to interprete and pass them from generation to generation. The symbols and designs have specific pronunciation, meaning, and usage. However, they are different from modern writings, and can only be regarded as a kind of primitive writing device.

帕孜《送魂经》

《送魂经》是纳木依人用来给过世的老人送魂的一种图画经。图中记载了纳木依祖先的迁徙路线。《送魂经》非常神圣，平时不能轻易打开，只有做送魂道场时，才由纳木依祭司帕孜打开。开图时要经过一系列的复杂程序，如宰杀牲畜、给神敬酒、唱经、摇铃等。

The Pazis' *Itinerary Map*

The Pazis' *itinerary map*, is used for seeing off the souls of the deceased ancestors. The map indicated the migration routes of the ancestors of the Namuzi pepole.

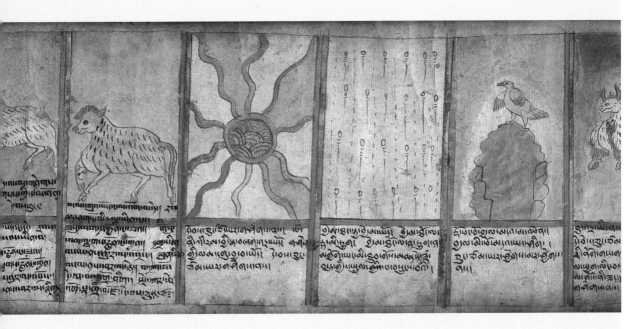

纳木依历书

　　纳木依历书，采用的是周代历法，即以夏历的十一月为正月，每月只有 30 天，一年共 360 天。每一年、每一月、每一天都有属相，按照十二生肖的顺序排列。纳木依帕孜根据历书中每年、每月、每天的属相来判断吉凶，为病人除病解灾。

　　纳木依历书体现了纳木依人信仰中的多神崇拜现象，每一种神鬼都与人们的生老病死有密切的关系，而纳木依历书上五颜六色的图案，就是人们敬神拜鬼、消灾解难的重要依据。

The Almanac of the Namuzi people

The Namuzi almanac followed the calendar system of the Zhou dynasty. Its First month is equal to the eleventh month in the lunar calendar. There are only 30 days in every month of their almanac, so one year has 360 days. Each year, month and day has asymbolic animal arranged by the order of the Chinese zodiac signs. The pazi determines the auspicious and inauspicious signs based on the zodiac signs of the days, months and years, and it also applied to the patients whose illness was expected to be cured off and misfortunes to be removed.

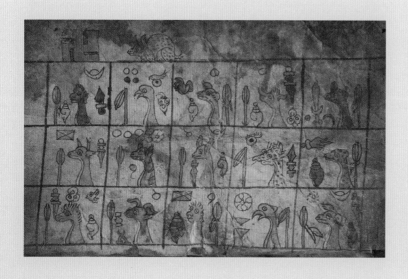

纳木依印棒

The Namuzis' Yin Bang

　　纳木依印棒，用樱桃木刻制而成的祭祀用品，主要用途是在祭祀用的糌粑上印出图案，糌粑在祭祀场合送神送鬼时使用。

木雅经书

　　木雅（Min-Yag）人，属于康巴藏族支系之一，主要居住在四川康定以西、雅江以东、道孚以南、九龙以北、丹巴西南这一片地区。他们说木雅语，被称为"木雅人"。他们是西夏党项羌一个部落辗转迁移而延续下来的后裔，既保留了党项羌先祖的文化遗产，又受到藏、彝、汉族等民族文化的深刻影响，故木雅文化呈现丰富、复杂、独特的面貌。

The Muyas' Scriptures

The Muya (Min-yag) people belong to an ethnic sub-group of the Khampa Tibetans. They mainly live in the regions of western Kangding, southern Dawu, eastern Yajiang, northern Jiulong and southwestern Danba in Sichuan Province. Their native speech is Muya, and hence they are called the Muya people .

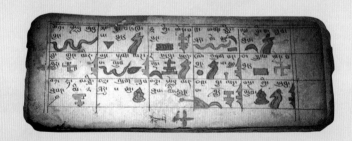

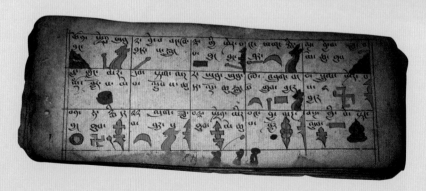

木雅历书

　　木雅历书，同耳苏、普米、纳木依、摩梭等历书一样，是"看日子的书"，根据天象历法推算择日，是日常使用最多的经书之一。历书共有 12 个月，每页半个月，每一个月 2 页，共 30 小格，即 30 天，一共 360 天。

The Almanac of the Muya people

The Muya almanac is the scripture for Muya priests to choose auspicious days, according to celestial phenomena.

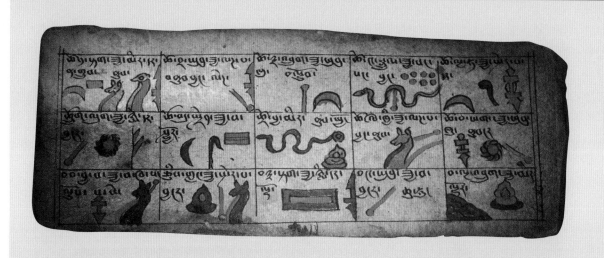

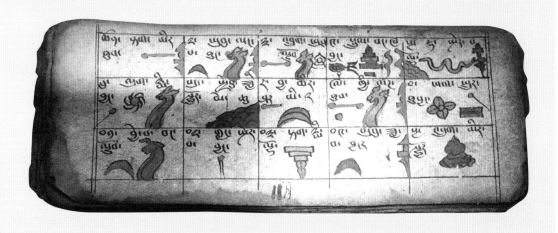

打卦图

用木雅的藏文写作：ᨖᨕ，读为 mu²¹ tɕɛ⁵¹。一共四本，每本九页，上面分别写着ᨕᨔᨕᨖ（藏文前四个字母）。使用时按顺序拼在一起，用于择日。打卦图的主要用途是测算这一天的好坏，多用于求财时测算这一天中是否有财运。使用时根据被测者的八字、属相等进行计算。

The Divination Painting

The main purpose of such a painting is used to predicate the good or ill luck of particular day by the testee's zodiac sign or the specific time of one's birthday. Normally it is used to decide whether a day is likely to be good for making money.

四、彝族

彝族是一个具有悠久历史的民族，居住在云南、四川、贵州等地。经过长期的历史发展，因方言和地域差异，加上社会历史的变化和自身不断发展等诸多因素，形成了比较多的彝族支系，也留存了大量的文字文献。

IV. The Yis

Distributed over Yunnan, Sichuan and Guizhou provinces, the Yis have a long-standing history. Due to differences in their dialects, regions, and history of development, they are divided into different ethnic sub-groups.

毕摩文献

清华大学图书馆藏毕摩古彝文写本文献，共 2100 余册，由民族学家马学良先生（1913—1999）于 20 世纪 40 年代在云南武定、禄劝一带主持收集。曾由北平图书馆和北大、清华、南开三校及中央研究院史语所共同保藏，而中央研究院保存的一部分在 1949 年被运往台湾。

修复后的毕摩文献
Restored Bimo Documents

清华大学图书馆藏古彝文典籍共有：刻本1册、写本及传抄本251册。成书年代从明末到民国二三十年代，以清写本居多。开本各异，大者长逾200厘米、宽约60厘米，版面小者近似汉文古籍的巾箱本，仅高9厘米、阔6厘米。各册页数多寡不一，多者300余页，少者不足10页。行文款式，大多数保持彝文的行文传统，从上往下、从左至右的直书式；少部分受汉文影响，改为从上往下、从右至左的直书式。装帧多为布面裹卷装，是这些古籍特有的一种近似线装的装帧方式。从内容上看，除宗教经书外，还有家谱、医书、史书、唱本、天文历算等。

2004年，清华大学图书馆请中央民族大学彝文专家进行了初步整理，并请天津图书馆历史文献部进行了科学修复。在2008—2010年公布的三批《国家珍贵古籍名录》上，共收录了九部清华彝文书，被认定为"国家级珍贵古籍"。

Bimo documents (collection of Tsinghua University Library)

The total number of hand-written literature of Ancient Yi scripts in Tsinghua University Library is over 2,100 volumes. They were mainly collected by the ethnologist Ma Xueliang (1913-1999) in the 1940s across Wuding and Luchuan in Yunnan Province. Apart from the religious books, the collection covers genealogies, medical books, history records, librettos, ephemerides, etc. Nine of these documents in Tsinghua Library were included in the list of National Rare Ancient Books, and are considered as rare ancient books "on the national level".

未修复的毕摩文献
Original Bimo Documents

灵牌上的铎系文
The Duoxi Scripts on Spirit Tablets

他留铎系文

　　他留人，是彝族的一个支系，主要生活在云南省丽江永胜县六德傈僳族彝族乡。他留人的祭司称铎系。铎系文主要用于丧葬仪式中。他留丧葬仪式中，铎系舞蹈的同时，口唱铎系经，手写铎系文。铎系要在棺材两旁的灵牌上书写（画）一套图画性极强的固定符号（铎系文），书写每个符号时都要唱出一大段与之相关的内容。目前能使用这种图符的铎系寥寥无几。

The Duoxi Scripts of the Taliu People

The Taliu people belong to an ethnic sub-group of the Yis. They live mainly in Liude Township of Yongsheng County, Yunnan Province. The local priests are called Duoxi. The Duoxi scripts are mainly used in funeral rites.

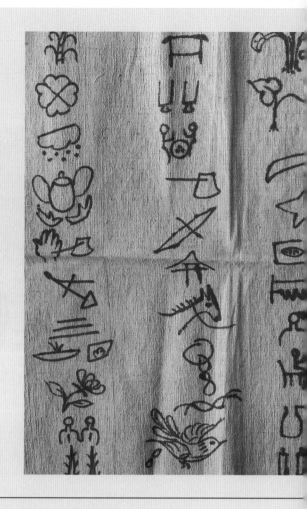

五、壮族

壮族主要分布在广西、云南、广东、湖南、贵州、四川等省区。以广西最多，其中云南主要聚居在文山州。壮族有自己的文字，是模仿汉字"六书"造字法而创造的一种与壮语语音一致的"方块壮字"。7世纪时就开始在民间使用，称为古壮字。由于使用面不广，没有能在全民推行，多用于书写地名、编山歌、记事等。

V. The Zhuangs

The Zhuangs live scattered in Guangxi Autonomous Region, Yunnan, Guangdong, Hunan, Guizhou and Sichuan Provinces. Formerly they had their a writing system for place-names, folk songs and historical records.

坡芽歌书

　　坡芽歌书是2006年在云南省文山壮族苗族自治州富宁县剥隘镇坡芽村发现的，是一套专用于记录情歌的图符文字。一共81个符号，每个符号代表一首歌，记录了从相识、相交、相知、相爱、发誓永不分离的整个过程，被誉为情爱教材。周有光先生为其定位为"文字之芽"。

The Poya Geshu

The Poya Geshu was found in Poya Village, Bo'ai Town, Funing County in the Wenshan Zhuang and Miao Autonomous Prefecture of Yunnan Province. It is a set of symbols used to record local love songs. There are 81 symbols, each standing for a song about acquaintance, contacts, understanding, loving and solemn promise to stay together. Therefore it is valued as a love textbook.

六、傈僳族

　　傈僳族是主要聚居在云南省怒江傈僳族自治州。傈僳族先后使用过西方传教士创制的拼音文字、汪忍波音节文字，现在使用新中国成立后创制的拉丁字母形式的新文字。

VI. The Lisus

Lisu People live in the Nujiang Lisu Autonomous Prefecture, Yunnan Province. Formerly the local people used an alphabetical writing system prepared by the visiting Western missionaries, later it was replaced by the Wang Renbo syllabic system. What is currently in use there is a new type of Latin alphabetical system since 1950s.

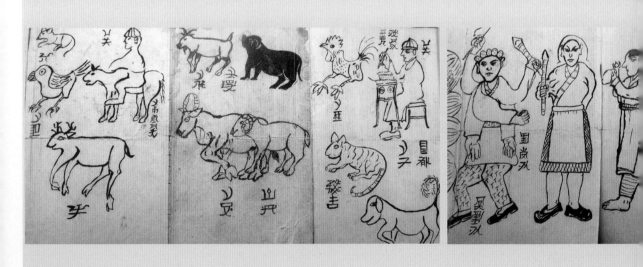

汪忍波音节文字抄本
The Hand-copied Wang Renbo syllabic characters

汪忍波音节文字

汪忍波音节文字，是近代史上明确由某人创制的一种文字。汪忍波（1900—1965），云南维西普通农民，自己一人用几十年的时间创制了一套音节文字，并着力傈僳族中加以推广、普及，曾在傈僳族地区流行一时。

Wang Renbo Syllabic Characters

Wang Renbo syllabic characters were created by Wang Renbo, a villager in Weixi County, in the 1920s~1930s. These characters were once popular among the Lisu people, but the number of the users now is small.

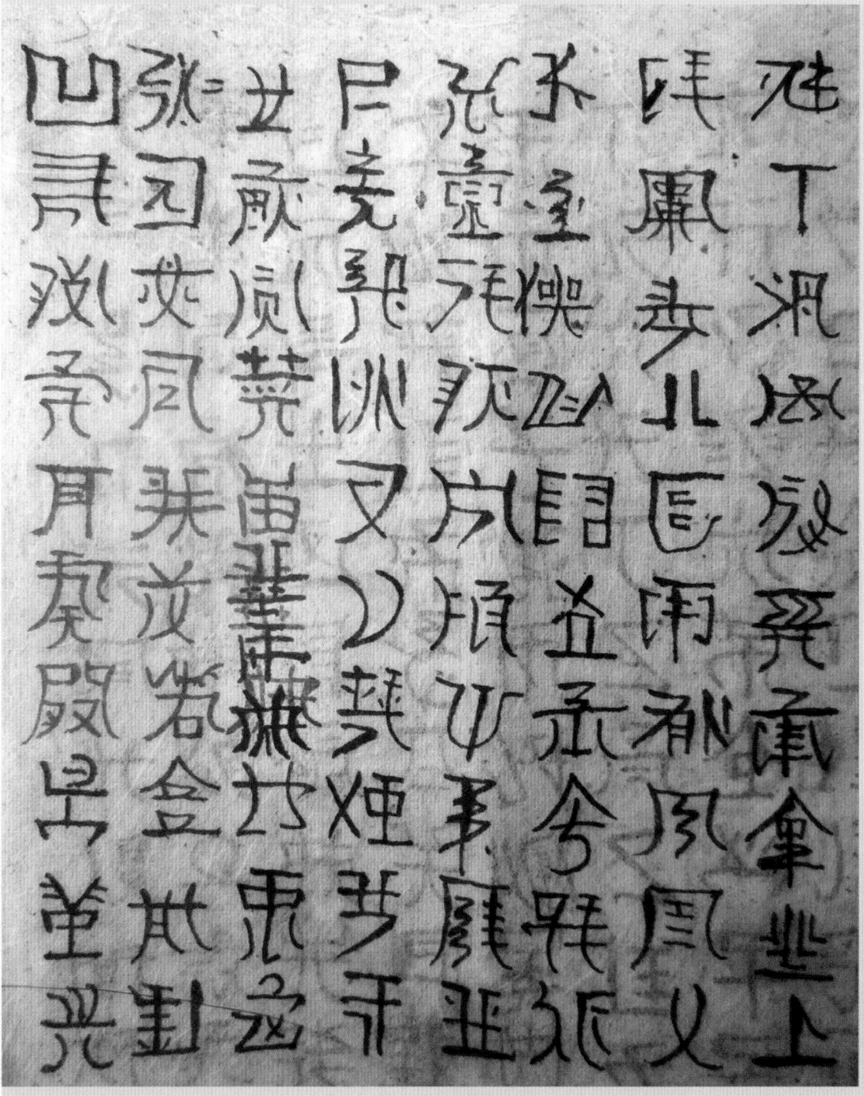

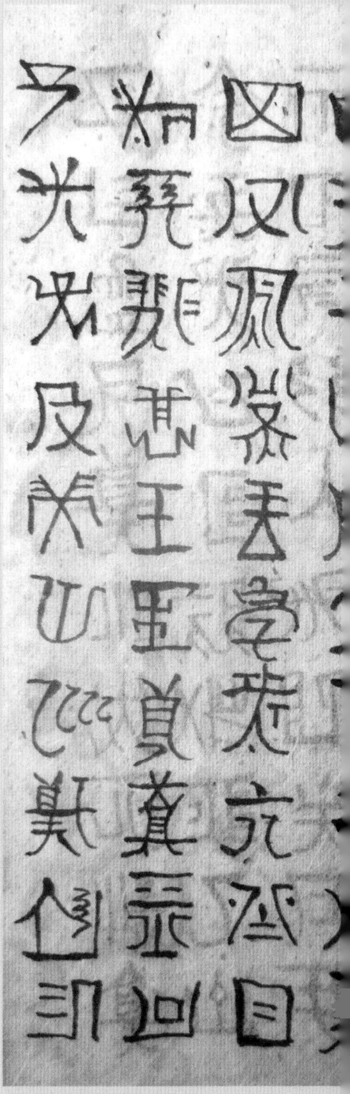

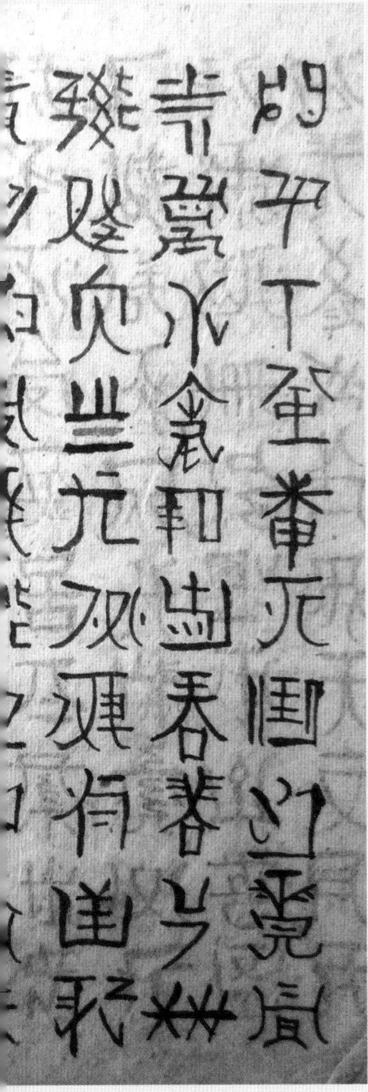

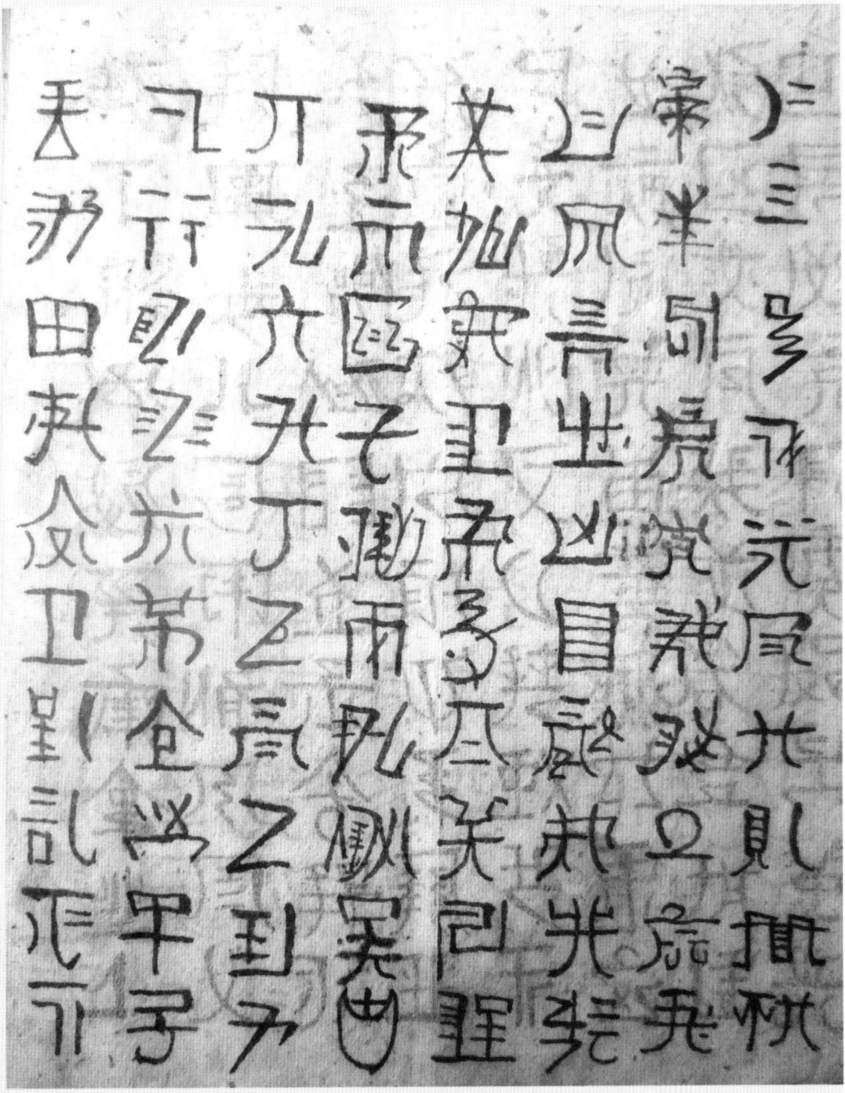

七、水族

　　水族主要生活在贵州省三都、荔波、独山、都匀一带。水族原有一种古文字，称为"水书"，现在则通用汉文。

VII. The Shuis

The Shuis mainly inhabit in Sandu, Libo, Dushan and Duyun Counties of Guizhou Province. Formerly they had their own writing system that has been replaced by the commonly-used Chinese characters.

水书

　　水书是水族的古文字。水书文字体系主要由借用、变异汉字及少量图符文字构成，尚不能完整记录语言。主要用于纪日、择吉避凶，如丧葬、婚嫁、营造、驱邪祈福等。

Shuishu

The Shuishu (script of Shui people) contains the Shuis' ancient scripts. It is composed of Chinese scripts, Chinese character variants and a few icons. It cannot record the entire language. It is used to count days and help people to pursue good fortunes and avoid the inauspicious. People use this book to choose days to carry out burials, hold weddings, build new houses and pray to their ancestors.

水书抄本
The Hand-copied Version of Shuishu

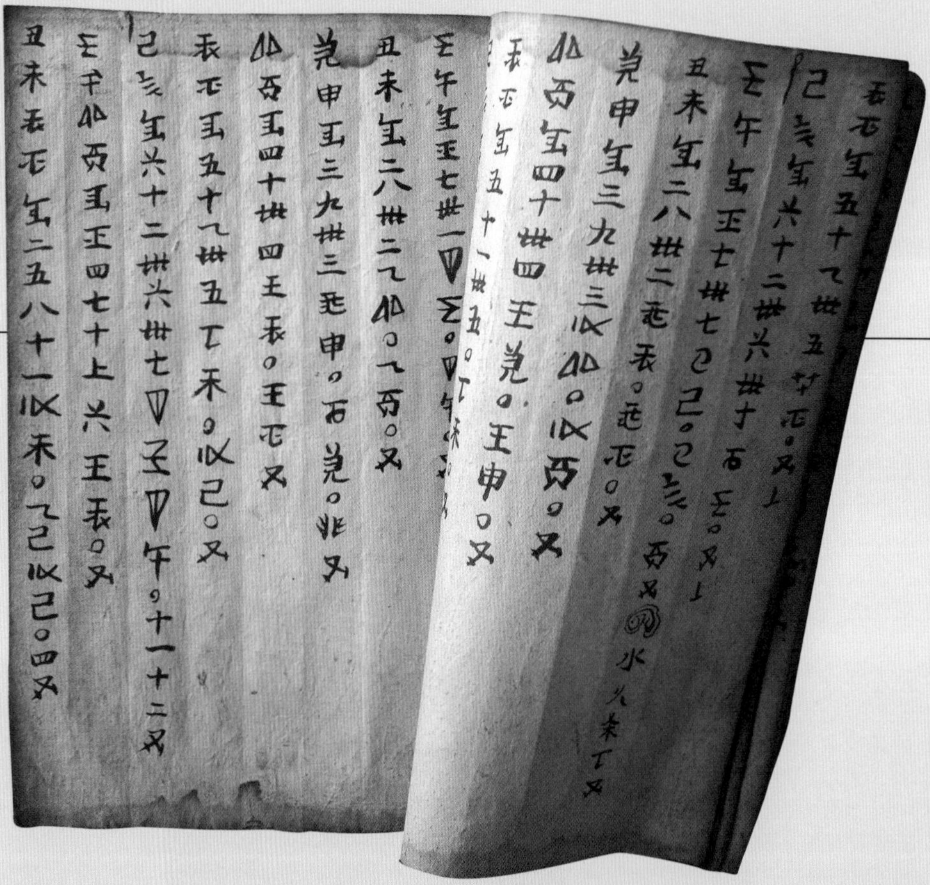

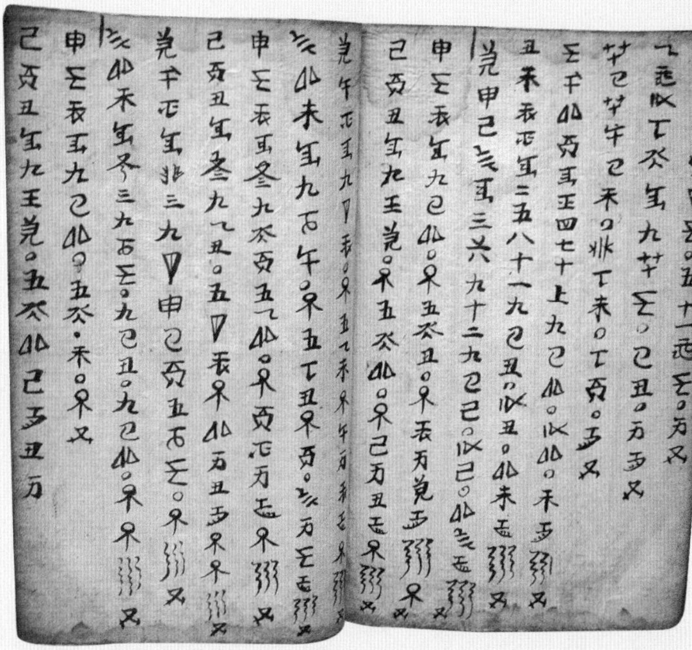

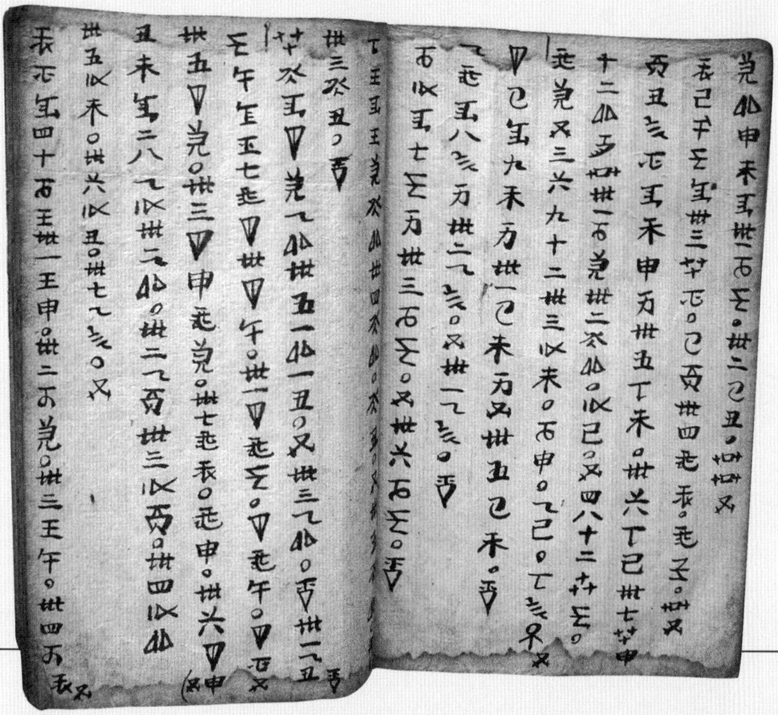

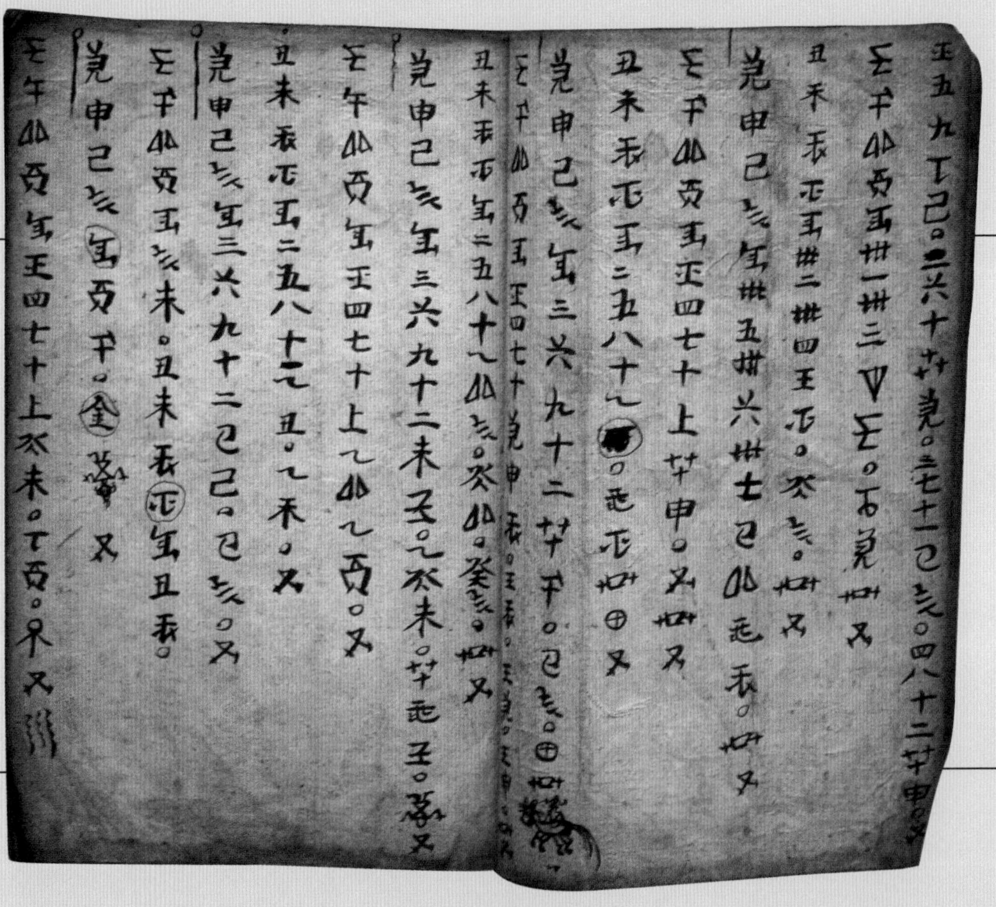

八、附录

VIII. Appendix

女书

　　女书，主要流传在湖南江永东北的潇水流域，是汉字的一种变体。女书是当地农家妇女专用文字，但不保密。当地一语二文，男人使用男字（方块汉字），女人使用女书。清华大学"抢救女书小组"对近千篇 20 世纪前女书作品的整理统计表明，女书基本字不到 400 个，是音节表音文字，主要通过同音／近音假借的方法，可以基本完整记录当地汉语方言土话。作品内容为写传诉苦、记录民歌、转写汉文唱本诗文等，反映当地男耕女织生活的方方面面。

Nüshu

Nüshu (script of Jiangyong women) are variants of Chinese characters, which mainly spreads around the districts near Xiaoshui River, northeastern of Jiangyong County of Hunan Province. Nüshu is a special script only used by the local rural women; however, it is not a secret for other people. The 400 basic phonetic characters in Nüshu can be used to record most of the local Chinese dialects or speeches.

婚嫁时的礼物三朝书

Sanzhao Shu, the Gift for Marriage

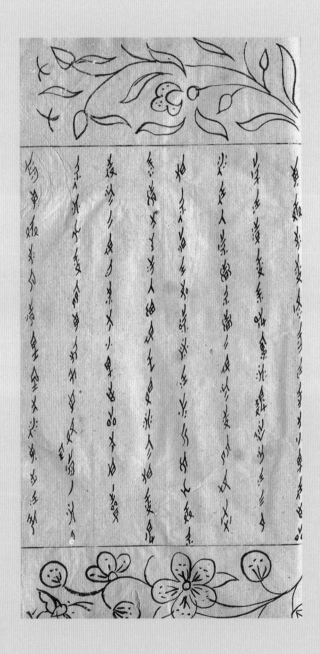

铜币上的女书

The Nüshu Copper Coin of Taiping Heavenly Kingdom

这是 20 世纪末在南京发现的太平天国铜币，"天下妇女，姊妹一家"。

It bears the phrase of "Women in the world are sisters in a family".

女书书法作品（一）

Nüshu Script I

这是写在扇面上的结拜姊妹的书信。

Letters on the fan

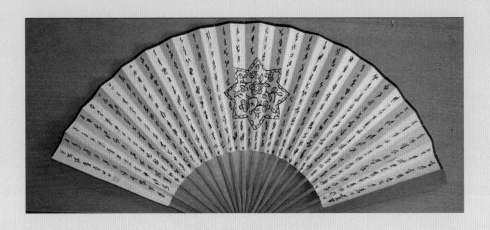

女书书法作品（二）

Nüshu Script II

这是用女书转写的唐诗《登鹳雀楼》《静夜思》。

Writing of Tang poems *Deng Guanque Lou* and *Jingye Si*.

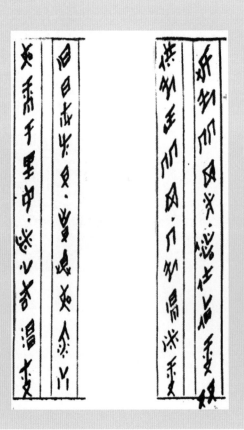

鸣 谢

　　幸逢清华百年，举办"中国西南濒危文字展"，首先要感谢百年来清华人开创的清华精神：求实、求是、创新；感谢清华大学文科处的辛勤工作；感谢校图书馆、人文学院以及中文系的大力支持。

　　特别要感谢中国国家博物馆研究员宋兆麟先生数十年田野考古的执着和鼎力支持；更要感谢接受我们采访、提供资料的濒危文字的传承人和单位团体，他们是东巴研究院、丽江博物院、丽江茶马古道博物馆、白地东巴传习所、宝山吾木东巴传习院、鲁甸东巴传习院、摩梭研究会、普米研究会、永胜六德他留文化研究中心、西昌学院、凉山州民语委、维西县民委和维西县文化局，以及油米东巴和群众、纳木依祭司、木雅祭司、汪忍波后人、玛丽玛莎人等，没有他们，就不会有这样丰富的、立体活态的展览。

　　还要感谢满怀爱国热情的清华学子们。这是他们向祖国、向人民交出的一份完美答卷。

　　最后要感谢学苑出版社的编辑们，他们用高度的文化责任感和汗水"抢出"了这本书。

编 者

Acknowledgements

The Exhibition of Endangered Scripts in Southwest China is held on the great occasion of Centenary Celebration of Tsinghua University. It's the Tsinghua spirits of reality-seeking, correctness-seeking and innovating pioneered by Tsinghua students in the past century that encourages us to carry out such fieldworks and hold the exhibition. We sincerely appreciate the hard work of Humanities and Social Science Administration Office of Tsinghua University and the great support of Tsinghua University Library, School of Humanities and Social Sciences and Department of Chinese Language and Literature.

Moreover, high tributes should be particularly paid to Mr. Song Zhaolin from the Research Institute, National Museum of China, who has devoted himself to field archaeology for decades and supported us with kind efforts. We would also like to extend our sincere gratitude to the following people and organizations for their help:

Dongba Research Institute, Lijiang Museum, Training Institute of Baidi Dongba Culture, Training Institute of Baoshan Wumu Dongba Culture, Training Institute of Ludian Dongba, Mosuo Research Institute, Pumi Research Institute, Research Center for Yongsheng Liude Taliu Culture, Xichang College, Liangshan Ethnic Language Commission, Weixi Ethnic Affairs Commission, Weixi Bureau of Culture, masses of Youmi Dongba, Namuzi priests, Muya priests, successors of Wang Renbo, Malimasha people, and all the people who have helped us. Without the interviews with them and the materials supplied by them, we would not have been able to make such an abundant and vivid exhibition.

In addition, we would like to thank the Tsinghua students who are full of passion, patriotism, talent and professionalism. The catalog is their dedication and devotion to the motherland and to the people.

Finally, we would like to express our appreciation to the editors of the Academy Press. They have completed the book within incredible schedule with their sweat and high sense of culture responsibility.

Editor

Translated by Huang Tengyu, Li Minghua, Xu Duoduo and members of the SRT Group of The Endangered Scripts in Southwest China,
Tsinghua University
Revised by Anna Gurevich